HELLO

I'm *Geronimo Stilton*'s sister. As I'm sure you know from my brother's bestselling novels, I'm a special correspondent for *The Rodent's Gazette*, Mouse Island's most famouse newspaper. Unlike my 'fraidy mouse brother, I absolutely adore traveling, having adventures, and meeting rodents from all around the world!

The adventure I want to tell you about begins at Mouseford Academy, the school I went to when I was a young mouseling. I had such a great experience there as a student that I came back to teach a journalism class.

When I returned as a grown mouse, I met five really special students: Colette, Nicky, Pamela, Paulina, and Violet. You could hardly imagine five more different mouselings, but they became great friends right away. And they liked me so much that they decided to name their group after me: the Thea Sisters! I was so touched by that, I decided to write about their adventures. So turn the page to read a fabumouse adventure about the

THEA SISTERS!

Colette

She has a passion for clothing and style, especially anything pink. When she grows up, she wants to be a fashion editor.

Paulina

Cheerful and kind, she loves traveling and meeting rodents from all over the world. She has a magic touch when it comes to technology.

Violet

She's the bookworm of the group, and she loves learning. She enjoys classical music and dreams of becoming a famous violinist.

THE THEA SISTERS

Nicky

She comes from Australia and is very enthusiastic about sports and nature. She loves being outside and is always ready to get up and go!

Pamela

She is a great mechanic: Give her a screwdriver and she'll fix anything! She loves pizza, which she eats every day, and she loves to cook.

Do you want to help the Thea Sisters in this new adventure? It's not hard — just follow the clues!

When you see this magnifying glass, pay attention: It means there's an important clue on the page. Each time one appears, we'll review the clues so we don't miss anything.

**ARE YOU READY?
A NEW MYSTERY AWAITS!**

THEA STILTON AND THE AMERICAN DREAM

WITHDRAWN

Scholastic Inc.

The publisher does not have any control over and does not assume any responsibility for author or third-party websites or their content.

Published by Scholastic Inc., *Publishers since 1920,* 557 Broadway, New York, NY 10012. SCHOLASTIC and associated logos are trademarks and/or registered trademarks of Scholastic Inc.

Stilton is the name of a famous English cheese. It is a registered trademark of the Stilton Cheese Makers' Association.

This book is a work of fiction. Names, characters, places, and incidents are either the product of the author's imagination or are used fictitiously, and any resemblance to actual persons, living or dead, business establishments, events, or locales is entirely coincidental.

ISBN 978-1-338-68707-1

Text by Thea Stilton
Original title *Avventura negli U.S.A.*
Art director: Iacopo Bruno
Cover by Barbara Pellizzari, Giuseppe Facciotto, and Flavio Ferron
Illustrations by Barbara Pellizzari, Flavio Ferron, Giuseppe Facciotto, Chiara Balleello, Valeria Brambilla, Federico Giretti, and Antonio Campo
Graphics by Marti Lorini

Special thanks to AnnMarie Anderson
Translated by Lidia Tramontozzi
Interior design by Becky James

10 9 8 7 6 5 4 3 2 1   21 22 23 24 25

Printed in the U.S.A.   40
First printing 2021

READY TO GO!

It was dawn at Mouseford Academy. A light summer **BREEZE** fluttered through the open window, tickling Colette's nose.

The mouselet rolled over in bed and opened her eyes just enough to see the light filtering in from outside.

"Ugh." Colette sighed. "Is it time to get up already?" But then she smiled suddenly, sitting straight up in bed.

"Pam!" she called to her roommate. "Today's the day! We're finally **LEAVING**!"

But there was no answer.

"Pam?" Colette called out. She peered across

the room at the bed next to hers in the semidarkness.

The bed had been perfectly made and the **pajamas** were neatly folded. Colette noticed the two humongous **backpacks** by the door, packed and ready to go. They were in the exact spot where she and her friend had placed them the previous night.

"Where would she have gone so early?" Colette wondered aloud. Their flight didn't leave until the afternoon. She immediately texted the other **THEA SISTERS**. They hadn't seen Pam that morning, either!

"Maybe the excitement of the trip woke her early with a big appetite and she went straight to breakfast," Nicky said when she, Violet, and Paulina joined Colette a few minutes later.

"That could be," Paulina replied, smiling. "She's probably waiting for us in the cafeteria right now, ready for a second breakfast!"

"Well, let's go find out if you're right!" Colette said.

Her friends followed Colette out of the mouselets' bedroom and into the deserted hallway. Then they scurried toward the cafeteria.

Summer **Vacation** had started a few days ago, and most of the students had already left, so the campus was unusually quiet.

The four friends were right outside the cafeteria when they heard a voice from inside.

"We'll land in **CHICAGO** and our road trip will begin from there!" Pam squeaked excitedly.

Colette, Nicky, Paulina, and Violet stepped into the cafeteria. Pamela had a map of the **United States** laid out on a table, and she was using cups, saucers, and cutlery to show Craig and Shen the itinerary for their trip.

"We'll rent a camper and drive across the country from east to west along the famouse **ROUTE 66**," Pamela continued. She pointed at the map with a teaspoon to highlight the

route. "And after crossing eight states, we'll arrive at our final destination, SANTA MONICA, California!"

"Pam, you're here!" Colette cried.

Pamela's snout lit up when she saw her friends.

"I'm so sorry I didn't wait for you to have breakfast," she explained hurriedly. "But I was too excited to stay in bed!"

"Don't worry," Violet reassured her, "that's what we figured!"

"We know you've being dreaming of this TRIP for years," Nicky added.

"I can understand why you couldn't sleep any longer," Colette agreed. "Who could sleep knowing that the next day would be the beginning of a

DREAM COME TRUE!"

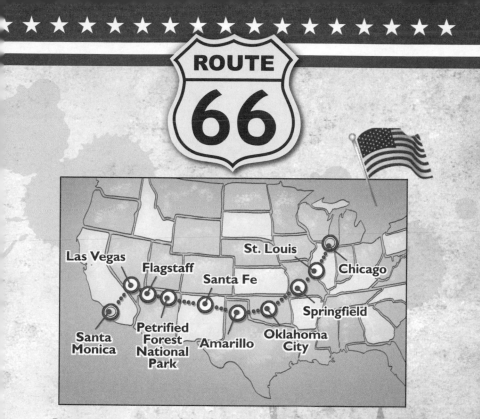

ROUTE 66

Las Vegas
Flagstaff
St. Louis
Chicago
Santa Fe
Springfield
Santa Monica
Petrified Forest National Park
Amarillo
Oklahoma City

Route 66 was one of the first interstate highways in the United States. The route was officially created in 1926 and ran for 2,448 miles (3,939 km) from Chicago, Illinois, to Santa Monica, California. Route 66 crosses eight states: Illinois, Missouri, Kansas, Oklahoma, Texas, New Mexico, Arizona, and California. During the 1950s and 1960s, Route 66 became popular with American families and was featured in songs, TV shows, and movies. Over the years, Route 66 has been replaced by newer highway systems. Today, tourists can still drive along about 85 percent of the original Route 66, visiting historical highlights and attractions that lie along this world-famous route.

A DREAM COME TRUE

The Thea Sisters had hatched the plan for their upcoming adventure on the most famous highway in the United States the previous spring. They had just gone to see a movie together that featured a family traveling on Route 66 in a **recreational vehicle**.*

"How I'd love to go on a road trip in an **RV** with my best friends." Pamela sighed as she and her friends came out of the theater.

"Well, why don't we?" Nicky asked.

"Yes, great idea!" Violet agreed.

Colette nodded, and Pamela began excitedly planning the trip later that day!

* Also called an RV, a recreational vehicle is a van equipped with beds, a small kitchen, and a bathroom so tourists can live in it while traveling.

In the months that followed, the five friends planned everything down to the smallest detail: the plane tickets, the route, and the places they would stay. But most of all, they fantasized about the **unforgettable** sites they would visit. Now that they had landed

in Chicago, their journey would finally begin. Or would it?

"I'm sorry, but your RV isn't ready yet," explained the mouse at the rental counter where the Thea Sisters had booked the vehicle.

"Our mechanics are finishing the final **checkup**," the clerk explained. "You can come back and pick it up this afternoon."

Pamela sighed as she and her friends left the rental office. "I can't wait to get my paws on that steering wheel and hit the road!"

★ CHICAGO ★

Chicago is the largest city in Illinois, with a population of more than two and a half million people. The city sits right on the shores of Lake Michigan and is famous for its iconic architecture and skyline. One of the city's most popular nicknames is "The Windy City."

"Well, why don't we look at the positive side of things," Nicky suggested. "We could visit **CHICAGO**!"

"Sure, but it's a big city and we have less than a day to explore," Violet said hesitantly as she flipped through her tourist guidebook. "How will we decide what to see?"

"It's too bad we don't know anyone who lives around here," Colette remarked. "If we had friends nearby, they could suggest some can't-miss places!"

Pamela smiled.

"It's true that we don't have any friends living here, but that doesn't mean we can't get **advice** from those who know the city well!" she squeaked.

Colette, Violet, Nicky, and Paulina gave her a puzzled look.

"But who?!" they asked in unison.

"The **mice** of Chicago, of course!" Pamela exclaimed, pointing to the crowded street. Then she turned to Colette.

"What would you like to see, Coco?" she asked.

"Hmmm, I guess after so many hours on the plane, I would love to stretch my paws a

bit **OUTDOORS**," Colette mused thoughtfully. "But I'd also like to see some **art**. I can't make up my mind!"

"Sounds good," Pamela said. "I'm on a mission!"

She headed toward a nearby hot dog stand, a huge smile on her snout. After a few minutes spent chatting with the two vendors running the stand, she returned to her friends, waving a **MAP** of Chicago.

"According to them, we aren't far from the perfect place to explore the outdoors and see some art: **Millennium Park!**"

The five mousclets followed the directions from the hot dog cart vendors and soon found themselves in an immense **PARK** between towering skyscrapers and sparkling Lake Michigan. The Thea Sisters quickly discovered the famous **Cloud Gate**, a

silver sculpture that mirrors the sky and the city's skyline. They learned that Chicagoans have nicknamed the sculpture "The Bean" thanks to its shape.

The Thea Sisters also loved the unique Crown Fountain, which consists of two glass towers on either side of a shallow pool of water. Video images of the faces of Chicagoans are projected on the two towers, which are built to create the illusion that water is flowing from the faces' mouths.

After spending some time walking among the many sculptures that made the park an open-air art gallery, Violet spotted a mouselet walking a dog and asked her to suggest a spot in Chicago a book lover might enjoy.

"Oh! You should go to the Chicago Cultural Center," the mouse replied. "It was the first public library in the city."

The mouse gave them directions and the Thea Sisters set out toward their next destination. The **Chicago Cultural Center** was a multistory building that hosted numerous book presentations and cultural events. Inside, the Thea Sisters admired the large **stained-glass** Tiffany dome set into the ceiling.

"What a wonderful place!" Violet exclaimed after they had explored the beautiful building.

"This has been such a fun morning!" Paulina exclaimed. "Where to now?"

Pam looked at the clock and smiled.

"According to my stomach, it's lunchtime," she said. "And I already know

exactly where to go!"

MEMORIES ON THE ROAD

To really get to know a new place, Pamela has to taste its *typical dishes*. That's why she took her friends to a restaurant where she knew she could sample a classic Chicago-style **pizza**.

"Wow!" Nicky exclaimed, wide-eyed as their server brought a steaming pie to their table. "I've never seen a pizza like *that* before!"

"That's because this is a **DEEP-DISH** pizza," Pamela said, smiling. "It's baked in a deeper pan, giving the crust a tall edge. That means there's lots of room for

Deep-dish pizza

extra cheese and a chunky tomato sauce. I've heard a lot about it, and I can't wait to taste it!"

"Yum!" Colette said as she bit into a slice. The pizza looked more like a piece of pie than a flatbread-style Italian pizza.

"This is **delicious**," Nicky added as she reached for a second piece of the pie.

Once the Thea Sisters had finished their pizza, it was Nicky's turn to choose their destination. She decided to ask their server for a suggestion.

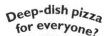

Deep-dish pizza for everyone?

"What's the perfect thing to do in **CHICAGO** for a mouse who loves the outdoors?" Nicky asked.

"Well, on a sunny day like this, I would take a boat ride," she replied.

"What a pawsome idea!" Nicky exclaimed.

Shortly after that, the Thea Sisters boarded a **boat** that sailed first on Lake Michigan and then down the Chicago River. Along the way, they admired the city's many beautiful buildings.

"Smile!" Colette told her friends as she snapped a photo just before the boat went under one of Chicago's famous movable bridges.

"This is a great photo of all of us!" Paulina said happily as she looked at the photo on Colette's phone. "I'll print it out as soon as we get on the RV!"

Colette frowned.

"But how will you do that?" she asked Paulina, a confused look on her snout. "I don't think the RV we rented has a **printer!**"

"Don't worry," Paulina revealed with a grin. "I brought my own! It's the latest model of portable mini printers. I figured for a trip on the legendary ROUTE 66, digital photographs just wouldn't do. Now we can create a real album of our memories on the road!"

"What a fun idea!" Violet squeaked in response. "When we get back to **MOUSEFORD ACADEMY**, we can show it to our friends."

"You should print one for each of us so we can carry it around in our wallets!" Nicky said.

Once back onshore, it was Paulina who suggested the LAST STOP on their impromptu tour of Chicago.

"I don't need to ask for suggestions," Paulina admitted. "During the boat ride, I overheard some tourists talking about the perfect spot to get a panoramic view of the entire city: **WILLIS TOWER**!"

The Thea Sisters headed for the skyscraper, which is famous for its Skydeck on the 103rd floor.

"Wow!" Violet exclaimed as she stepped out of the ELEVATOR. "Look at that view!"

Colette pulled out her guidebook. "It says here that beyond the lake, you can see the states of Indiana, Michigan, and Wisconsin," she read. "This really is an extraordinary **VIEW**!"

But the excitement wasn't over. The Thea Sisters noticed some special enclosed GLASS balconies that extended out

What a view!

more than four feet past the building, giving them a view of Chicago as if they were suspended 1,353 feet in the air!

"That was quite a thrill," Colette said.

Pamela glanced at her watch as they took the elevator back to the ground level.

"It's almost time to pick up the RV," she announced. "But there's still a little time left for one LAST stop."

"Where is that?" Paulina asked, intrigued.

"A place where we'll get a very important **photo** for our album," Pam replied. "The road **SIGN** that marks the start of the historic Route 66!"

LET'S HIT THE ROAD!

The long-awaited moment had finally arrived. After picking up the keys to the RV, the Thea Sisters climbed aboard and officially began their all-American road trip!

Leaving Chicago behind, the mouselets headed southwest along Route 66. The skyscrapers of the city gave way to the plains of Illinois.

"Wow!" Colette said, admiring the **VIEW** out the window. "This countryside seems to go on **forever**!"

"Get ready," Paulina squeaked. "We're about to make our first stop!"

"Welcome to **Pontiac, Illinois**!" Pamela said as she parked the RV.

The five friends hopped outside, excited to stretch their paws. They were ready to learn more about Route 66, so they headed straight for the redbrick building that housed the **Illinois Route 66 Hall of Fame and Museum**. The building had once housed Pontiac's fire department, but it had since been converted into a museum dedicated to the history of Route 66.

But the front door wouldn't open.

"It looks like it's closed!" Nicky grumbled, disappointed.

Violet looked up at the setting sun and then back down at the schedule they had plotted out weeks ago.

"According to our original itinerary, we were going to leave Chicago in the morning," she said. "Since we left later than planned, we've missed out on seeing the museum."

Paulina just shrugged.

"The beauty of making plans is that you can always make new ones!" she said.

"Well said, sister," Pamela agreed, nodding. "Why don't we spend the night here in Pontiac and visit the museum when it opens in the morning."

"Great idea," Colette agreed. "In the meantime, let's get a picture of the five of us together!"

She had stopped right in front of a large MURAL dedicated to Route 66. She realized her perfect shot wasn't going to happen.

"If I try to take a selfie with all five of us, the entire mural won't fit," Colette said, sighing.

"And we can't use the timer because we would have to put the camera in the middle of the road," Violet added.

But Colette wasn't going to give up so easily. She began looking around for someone who would take a picture of them. She finally spotted a brown-haired **mouselet** with a large backpack and a blue computer bag.

"Excuse me!" Colette called out to her. "Would you mind taking a **PICTURE** of us?"

Would you take a picture of us?

"A picture . . . um, sure!" the mouselet replied as she stifled a big yawn. "Just let me know when you're ready!"

The five friends had fun posing for their picture and thanked the mouse for her help. Then they headed to a local restaurant for

dinner before ending their first day on the road with a good night's sleep in the **RV**.

Bright and early the next morning, the Thea Sisters were ready to resume their journey.

"But first, it's time for breakfast!" Pamela announced as they walked into a coffee shop that smelled of fresh pancakes. Just as the mouselets sat down at a table, the door opened.

The mouselet with the blue computer bag they had met the previous day walked in. Without noticing the Thea Sisters, she headed straight for the table next to theirs, dropped into a booth, and sat there **crying**.

Paulina noticed and exchanged a glance with her friends. Then she leaned toward the table and spoke to the mouselet softly.

"Hi. Do you remember us?" she asked. "We met yesterday when you took our photo."

The stranger looked up and nodded sadly.

"We don't want to bother you, but you seem upset," Nicky said. "Is everything **OKAY**?"

As tears fell down her cheeks, the mouse shook her head.

"Would you like to **talk** about it?" Violet tried gently.

The mouselet stared at the Thea Sisters for a few moments in silence. Then she let out a *sigh* and began to tell her story . . .

AN UNEXPECTED TALE

The mouse with the blue computer bag was named Ali. She was the same age as the Thea Sisters and, like them, had decided to plan a special trip across the United States that summer. But unfortunately for Ali, her journey was not going as planned!

"When I left Detroit, I had a very specific plan," she explained. "I wanted to cross the United States from Detroit, Michigan, to San Jose, California, by **BUS**. Along the way, I had planned to stop and visit the most famous cities along Route 66.

"But before I even got on the road, my **schedule** had already fallen apart!"

Thanks to a series of unexpected events,

Ali had **missed** the bus in Detroit. She had to quickly change her **TICKETS**, and then she had spent long hours in bus stations instead of enjoying her adventure!

"You poor thing!" Colette remarked. "You looked *so tired* yesterday."

"That's because I had just arrived in Pontiac after a very long day," Ali explained.

Then her voice began to tremble. "And this morning I did it again! I was so tired I didn't hear my **alarm** go off, and I missed the bus to St. Louis!"

I even missed the bus to St. Louis!

The Thea Sisters looked at the mouse sympathetically. They could only imagine how disappointed Ali must have been!

"You said you're going to San Jose, but Route 66 doesn't end there," Nicky pointed out, trying to change the subject. "The route actually ends in **Santa Monica**."

"Yes, I know," Ali replied. "But in two weeks I have an important appointment in San Jose. My itinerary would have taken me there instead of to Santa Monica."

With a plate of steaming pancakes in front of her, Ali explained that she wanted to be a

video game programmer. She was going to try to make her dreams come true in San Jose.

"San Jose is thought of as the **CAPITAL** of Silicon Valley," Paulina said knowingly. She was really into computers, and so she knew all about that area of the country. "A lot of **computer** companies have their headquarters there!"

"That's right," Ali said, nodding as she poured a little maple syrup over her pancakes.

★ SILICON VALLEY ★

Silicon Valley is the nickname for the region near the San Francisco Bay Area in Northern California that includes the cities of San Jose, Palo Alto, Menlo Park, Redwood City, Cupertino, Santa Clara, Mountain View, and Sunnyvale. The nickname is due to the concentration of companies in the area that deal with computers, new technologies, and social media. Silicon is an important element in microelectronics and computer chips.

"And **Level Up** is one of those companies. Every year they give young programmers the opportunity to present a new video game to a group of investors. The best project presented will become a **REAL GAME!**"

"What an incredible opportunity!" Pamela exclaimed.

"I know!" Ali said, her eyes sparkling. "In fact, I spent the whole year studying and working on my video game. That's why I thought I'd treat myself to a **Vacation** before the presentation. But seeing how things are going, I think I'll head back home and just **fly** to California!"

The **THEA SISTERS** glanced at one another. The five friends could tell they were each thinking the same thing. It was Violet who finally spoke up on behalf of the group.

"What if we had a solution to your problem?" Violet asked.

"Yes, we don't think you should **GIVE UP** on your trip!" Nicky added.

"You can travel with us inside our comfortable **RV**!" Pamela exclaimed with a big grin.

Ali looked at the five mouselets in surprise.

"Really?!" she asked. "Are you saying I can continue my **TRIP** with all of you?"

"Of course!" Colette replied. "There's room for one more in the RV! And we have the same itinerary as you. We only have to add a little detour to get you to San Jose!"

Ali put down her **FORK** and looked at the Thea Sisters.

"California, here we come!" she shouted. Her eyes were filled with tears again. But this time, they were tears of **JOY**. She would be able to continue with her road trip, and this time she would be sharing it with

Five special new Friends!

An Old Friend

The Thea Sisters learned pretty quickly that Ali was a **perfect** traveling companion. She fit right in with the group. She had a passion for travel, and loved to see new places and sing songs from Paulina's playlist at the top of her lungs. The mouselet also proved to be an experienced copilot.

In fact, in order to follow the original **ROUTE 66**, the travelers couldn't rely on just the GPS. They also had to consult the guides and maps that marked every

Ali is the sixth voice in our RV chorus!

point of historical interest along the route, and Ali was very good at this. The mouselet soon gained Pamela's complete **trust**, along with the seat next to the driver!

"There should be a fork in the road in a couple of miles," Pam said to Ali. "Do you see it on the map?"

Pam took a quick look at the SCREEN of the cell phone fixed to the dashboard, where the route appeared. But Ali had put down the ROAD MAP and was sending a text on her cell phone.

"Ali?" Pamela asked again. "Did you hear me? You're my navigator. I need your eyes and ears!"

The mouselet snapped her head up, grabbed the map, and tried to get her bearings.

"I'm so sorry!" she said. "I got distracted for a second!"

"It's no big deal!" Pamela replied, laughing. Then she pointed to a red flashing light on the control panel. "We have to stop for **gas**, anyway. We can look over the map during the stop."

The mouselets stopped at the next station and grabbed some lemonades and stretched their paws.

"Pam, I'm sorry again about before," Ali said. "I shouldn't have gotten distracted by the phone. I just got incredible **news**

Hi!

from a friend I haven't heard from in a long time!"

Ali told the Thea Sisters that her friend was named Benji, and he had been a classmate back in Detroit. Benji was also a huge fan of computers and video games, and like Ali, he was studying COmputer science. Benji had left Detroit and enrolled in a college in St. Louis.

"After he moved, we lost touch," Ali continued. "He just sent me a message. It looks like he found out through a friend that I'm participating in the Level Up competition.

"He's also going to be there to present a project! He wants to meet up and say hello."

"What a coincidence!" Colette exclaimed.

"It will be so nice to have a friend there!"

"I know," Ali agreed with a nod. "He was one of my best friends, and I was sorry to have lost touch with him."

At that moment, Ali's phone **buzzed** again, and the screen lit up with a new **message**.

"It's Benji again," Ali said as she looked down at her phone. "I texted him about our trip along Route 66. He's wondering if we'd like to stop in St. Louis for a quick visit. He says he would love to show us around a little bit before hitting the road to the competition!"

"**St. Louis** is along the way, and it's not that far from here," Nicky remarked as she glanced at the map.

"How about it?" Paulina asked as she took the last sip of her drink. "I read that St. Louis is famous for **blues music**."

"It's fine by me!" Violet replied.

The other Thea Sisters agreed that a stop in St. Louis would be a great detour, so the group set off to meet Benji.

A few hours later, the Thea Sisters' RV sped along Route 66 and crossed their first state border. The mouselets said good-bye to Illinois and entered the state of **MiSSOURi**!

MEET ME IN ST. LOUIS

The Thea Sisters met up with Benji near the **Gateway Arch**, an impressive monument and symbol of St. Louis. The Thea Sisters looked up at the sixty-three-story arch in awe. What a feat of engineering!

A moment later Benji arrived, along with two other mice.

"Hi, Ali!" Benji greeted his friend warmly. "This is Phil and this is Jerry. They're my college roommates and **best friends**." Then he turned to the guys. "This is Ali, my good friend from Detroit."

"Oh, hi." Phil nodded. "Nice to meet you."

But the Thea Sisters noticed right away that Phil did not look happy.

"Benji says you're a computer genius," Jerry echoed in the same upset voice.

Ali didn't seem to notice how **cold** the two mice were being. She blushed at the compliment.

But Paulina leaned over to the other Thea Sisters.

"It doesn't sound like he means that," she whispered.

"Maybe they're just shy," Violet replied. "After all, they don't know us or Ali."

Phil and Jerry continued to sit apart from the rest of them, even when the group sat down to **chat** on some steps overlooking the Mississippi River. At one point, Phil pulled out a **BASEBALL GLOVE** from his backpack and asked his friend to play catch in the park behind them.

"Did someone say **baseball**?" Nicky exclaimed as she jumped up. Then, pretending to tie her shoe, she leaned over to her friends.

"Nothing like some SPORTS to break the ice," she whispered with a wink.

And she was right! Playing ball seemed to soften up Phil and Jerry. After throwing a few balls, they finally smiled!

What a pitch!

"Oh, oh!" Colette exclaimed as she ran to get a fly ball she had missed. "I'm afraid I haven't had much practice playing baseball!"

"That's okay," Benji said. "But Pam here is a great pitcher!"

Pamela smiled at the compliment.

"I was on the **baseball** team at my school in New York when I was a little mouseling," she explained.

★ BASEBALL ★

Baseball is one of the most popular sports in the United States. It dates back to the eighteenth century and likely developed out of two games brought to the country by English settlers: a children's game called rounders and the game of cricket. A group of men in New York City formed the first official team in September 1845 and named it the New York Knickerbocker Baseball Club.

"I didn't know that!" Nicky exclaimed. "When we get back to Mouseford Academy, we should organize a game one weekend."

"In the meantime, if you want to see a **baseball** game, you've come to the right place," Phil said. "The St. Louis Cardinals are playing today!"

Jerry looked at his watch. "If we hurry, we may still be able to get tickets!"

The group got to **BUSCH STADIUM** in no time, and the Thea Sisters and their new friends took their seats in the crowded stands.

"Ali told us you're presenting a video game at the Level Up competition, too," Paulina said to Benji as they waited for the game to start.

"Actually, it's *our* video game," Benji said **proudly** as he gestured toward his roommates. "Phil, Jerry, and I worked really hard on it. We're going to present it **together**!"

"Cool!" Paulina said.

"What kind of game is it?" Pam asked curiously.

Phil and Jerry turned to look at her in **shock**.

"We can't tell you that!" Phil cried out.

Jerry nodded furiously.

Benji noticed the confused looks on Pamela's and Paulina's snouts and hurried to explain.

"We worked really hard on this project," he said. "So we want to keep it a **surprise** until the day of the presentation!"

"Oh, of course!" Ali replied, chuckling. "Well, I don't have any secrets because Benji already knows the **VIDEO GAME** I'm presenting."

"Me?!" Benji asked in surprise. "But how would I know it?"

"Because I developed the idea for the video game we came up with for our high school graduation project: Power Princess," Ali replied. "I asked you if you wanted to continue working on it with me a few months ago.

I don't remember...

Don't you **remember**?"

I'm sorry. I don't have the time!

But Benji just shook his head, a BLANK look on his snout.

Ali reminded Benji how she had written to him months earlier and explained that she wanted to turn their idea into a real video game. She had asked Benji if he wanted to work on it with her, but he said that he didn't have the time. The pair hadn't been in touch since then.

"You're right," Benji admitted slowly. "I had completely forgotten. I'm **sorry** I said no, but you know how it is. I had just moved to St. Louis and I was so busy with schoolwork."

"Oh, don't worry," Ali reassured him. "I

understand. I finished it on my own, and I'm very happy with the result!"

At that moment, loud music blasted through the stadium speakers. The fans sprang to their feet as the TWO TEAMS came out onto the field, ready to begin the game.

For the next few hours, the Thea Sisters enjoyed watching the exhilarating game with their new friends. When it was over, they were sorry to have to say good-bye.

"What a shame we can't hang out a little longer," Benji said.

"That would be nice, but we really have to leave tomorrow," Nicky replied. "We'll see you soon for the Level Up presentations, though!"

"Of course!" Ali said as she hugged Benji good-bye. "See you soon!"

A SURPRISE STOP

As scheduled, the following **morning** the Thea Sisters and Ali woke up early, had a small breakfast, and set off in the RV. A little over an hour later, they were squeaking along with the radio as loud as they could when Ali's cell phone **buzzed**.

"It's a message from Benji," Ali announced as she turned the volume down and checked the screen. She read the text and frowned. "He asked if we've left yet."

It's Benji!

"I'd say so!" Pamela replied cheerfully. "We have to cross the entire state of Missouri, and then . . ."

Buzz! Buzz!

"It's Benji again," Ali said. "He's wondering if we can stop and . . . **WAIT**!"

"Wait for what?!" Violet asked, perplexed. "And why?"

Ali shook her head.

"I have no clue," she replied. "He says it's a surprise. What do you think? Should we stop? I know we are already behind the original schedule."

From the driver's seat, Pamela glanced at her friends in the rearview **MIRROR**. They were sitting on the RV's sofas, relaxing.

"Well, as you all know, I'm always ready for a second breakfast!" Pam said.

"Sure!" Paulina agreed. "We'll stop as soon as we can. Then we can find out what's going on."

Pamela pulled off the highway at the first

little town they came to. Ali texted Benji and let him know where they were.

Then the six mice entered a small, cozy diner and took seats in a booth near the window. They were welcomed by a friendly WAITER wearing an apron. "Good morning," he greeted them cheerfully. "What can I get you?"

"The PIES in the display case look very good," Colette said.

"They're delicious," Bob told them proudly. "My wife, Johanna, bakes them fresh every morning. Why don't I bring you a slice of each so you can taste them all?"

"Hey, I like this place!" Pam said with a smile as she anticipated the yummy-looking pies they were about to try.

As they waited for their order, the friends pulled out their ROAD MAPS and traced the next leg of their trip. But their thoughts kept returning over and over again to one **question**: Why had Benji asked them to stop?

"Maybe we left something in St. Louis and he wants to return it?" Violet guessed.

"Yes, but he would have just said that," replied Colette.

"Or . . . or . . . or . . ." pondered Nicky. "Or nothing! I just can't think of a reason!"

"Well, we're about to solve the mystery," Paulina said as she pointed out the window to a car that had just pulled into the diner's parking lot. "Here's Benji!"

"And there are Phil and Jerry, too," Colette noticed as Bob returned to the table with a tray full of dishes and began to distribute the slices of pie.

"Hey, guys!" Ali waved to the three young computer programmers as they entered the diner. "We've been waiting impatiently for you to arrive."

"Thanks for stopping." Benji smiled as he

approached the table. "Otherwise it would have taken us forever to catch up to you!"

"I think we need a little *explanation*," Ali told her friend.

"You're right, of course," Phil replied. "That *was* a little rude. We talked last night, and we decided we'd love to travel with you! That is, if you will have us."

"**Really?!**" Ali asked in surprise.

We'd like to go with you!

"It was Benji's idea," Jerry explained. "Since we also have to go to California, he thought it would be fun to take a **ROAD TRIP**, too!"

"What do you say?" Benji asked. "Can we follow your **RV** in our car?"

"Well, you can't come with

us right now," Pam replied, struggling to keep a straight snout. But after a moment, she laughed and pointed at the dishes in front of them. "First, we have to

FINISH ALL THIS DELICIOUS PIE!"

A MYSTERIOUS ATTACK

Soon the Thea Sisters and Ali were back on the road in the RV, followed by Phil, Jerry, and Benji in Benji's car. In the days that followed, the group of travelers crossed the state of **MiSSoURi** and passed through Kansas, arriving in Oklahoma, a state famouse for its Great Plains.

The group passed small towns that seemed to stand still in time, museums highlighting important moments in United States history, and many scenic landscapes along the **highway**.

The group of friends grew closer as they got to know one another better.

The ratlets were united by the same great

A real RV!

Direction: Adventure!

Having a whale of a time in Catoosa, Oklahoma!

passion as Ali: **video games**! After a few days together, the entire group had started using words that they had picked up from Benji, Phil, and Jerry.

"Guys, help me!" Paulina begged as she climbed aboard the RV **exhausted**. "My battery is run down!"

The camper was parked in a tree-lined campsite outside Oklahoma City where the group had decided to spend the night. Paulina had been driving all day, and she was ready for a rest.

"Hang in there." Ali giggled, pointing at the bed. "After a few hours, you'll be fully **recharged**!"

"I could use a bonus level of rest myself," Colette joked.

The tired mouselets went to bed, sleeping soundly. They woke the next morning to the sound of Ali's alarmed squeak.

"No, no, no!" Ali groaned. "Please turn on!"

Colette opened her eyes slowly.

"Huh?" she asked. "What's not turning on?"

"THE RV ISN'T TURNING ON?!" Pamela gasped as she woke with a start.

"No, not the RV," Ali replied. "It's my **computer!**"

The mouselet was seated on the floor with her laptop on her legs. "It shut down unexpectedly and now it doesn't want to turn back on again!"

Ali explained that she'd gotten up early

that morning to work on her **presentation**. But her computer stopped working all of a sudden!

"That's **weird**," Nicky said. "It was working just fine yesterday. I saw you using it!"

"I know, and everything was fine when I woke up this morning," Ali said with a sigh. "But then out of the blue . . . **puff**! First the screen froze and then it turned off completely!"

Their plans for the day were forgotten as everyone gathered around Ali's laptop. Benji, Phil, and Jerry left the cabin where they had been staying and **joined** the group as well.

"It's strange," Ali said. "This is a **brand-new** computer. I doubt there's something wrong with the hardware. The only thing I can think of is that someone tried to hack* into my computer!"

---

* To use technological knowledge to gain access to data in a computer system that isn't yours.

Paulina frowned. "Are you saying someone messed with your computer on purpose?" she asked.

Ali nodded.

"I think so," she said. "It's the only **POSSIBLE** explanation. The computer was working perfectly earlier!"

"But is it possible to do something like that?" Violet asked. "Without touching the computer?"

"Of course," Phil replied. "If Ali's computer was connected to the camp's Wi-Fi . . ."

". . . the **hacker** could have used it to gain access to her computer," Jerry concluded.

"I don't get it," Nicky objected. "**WHY** would someone do something like that? And why would they target **Ali**?"

Benji shrugged.

"Who knows?" he said. "There's no way to

know if the attack was directed at Ali. Hackers often act randomly, with the aim of hitting as many computers as possible."

"Oh, Ali, I'm so sorry," Colette said. She rushed over to **hug** her friend. "Was all

your work for the presentation on that computer?"

"Yes," Ali replied evenly.

Violet opened her eyes wide. "But how can you be so **calm**?" she gasped.

"Because I still have the copy I saved on my external memory drive," Ali explained. She rummaged through her bag and pulled out a charm in the shape of a **unicorn**!

"It's the pink unicorn from *Bubble Rainbow*!" Benji exclaimed. "I remember it! It was your favorite video game when we were little!"

"Yup! There's a **USB drive*** hidden inside," Ali revealed. "It's where all my data is stored.

"So I can still present my video game to **Level Up**!"

* A USB drive is a small, portable device that connects to a computer and stores data such as photos, audio files, documents, and computer programs.

"Awesome!" Pam said joyfully, happy that her friend still had a chance to make her dream come true. "That was a smart move. You must be so relieved!"

CLUE!

ALI'S LAPTOP CRASHED SUDDENLY. WAS IT A RANDOM HARDWARE PROBLEM, OR DID SOMEONE DELIBERATELY TRY TO HACK ALI'S COMPUTER FILES?

WELCOME TO TEXAS

The news that Ali's work was safe on her flash drive made everyone feel better. So the group returned to the task at paw: planning the next part of their road trip. Next stop: **Texas**!

After traveling for miles across boundless prairies dotted with ranches, the friends arrived in Amarillo. There, they decided to spend the night in one of the typical **MOTELS** that line Route 66.

"The receptionist told me they have three **triple rooms** for us," Colette said. "But, we have to wait until they finish cleaning them."

"That's okay," Paulina said. "We could use

the extra time to do some **SIGHTSEEING** around here!"

"Actually, we thought we'd use the time to go over our presentation," Phil said.

"But if our room isn't ready

ROUTE
66

AMARILLO
MOTEL

The rooms aren't ready yet!

yet, that will be hard to do," Jerry pointed out.

"You can use the **RV**," Violet suggested.

"That would be awesome. Thanks!" Benji replied. "What will you all do in the meantime?"

"We'll visit the city," Nicky replied. "What do you think, mouselets?"

"I would love to!" replied Ali. "I'm just going to put my **computer bag** in the RV, but first I have to . . . drat! Where did I put them?!"

Ali rummaged around in her bag.

"What are you looking for?" Pam asked.

"My **sunglasses**!" Ali replied as she pulled out most of the items in her bag. **"HERE THEY ARE!"**

She held up the glasses case and waved it victoriously.

Colette looked amused at the different things her friend had pulled out of her bag during the search.

"And I thought I had the most jam-packed **bag** in the world!" Colette said, laughing.

At that moment, a little mouse peeked out of the front door of the motel and noticed Ali's flash drive.

"Awesome!" he squeaked.

"You like **unicorns**, too?" Ali replied, smiling. She noticed that the mouse was

Awesome! May I see it?

hugging a stuffed unicorn.

Andrew, let's go!

"May I see it?" the young mouse asked. "I promise I won't break it!"

But at that moment, the mouse's mother came out of the motel.

"Andrew, come on, let's go," she said. "We have to hit the road!"

After saying good-bye to the little mouse, Ali gathered her things and put them back in her bag, which she left in the **RV**. Phil, Jerry, and Benji were just settling down to work on their presentation when Ali headed back outside to join the Thea Sisters.

The six friends made their way to one of the most popular attractions on Route 66: Cadillac Ranch! As soon as Pam saw the rows of graffiti-covered Cadillacs

sticking out of the ground, she broke into a huge grin.

"This is the most beautiful place on the trip so far!" Pam told her friends happily.

As she walked through the paint-splattered cars with her new friends, Ali had a moment of reflection.

"I'm really glad that my solo traveling plans fell apart," Ali said. "If everything had gone according to my plan, I would have never met the five of you!"

"We're happy, too," Colette agreed. "Happy to have met you, and glad that we will be accompanying you, Phil, Jerry, and Benji to your Level Up presentations!"

"You don't know how happy it makes me to see Benji again," Ali said. "I am glad we can encourage each other just like we did in school! Seeing him again is just like **old**

times. A few nights ago I told him how I developed the graduation project and turned it into a video game."

"Speaking of presentations, I wonder if the guys are finished yet," Violet said.

The six mice returned to the RV just as Benji, Phil, and Jerry were turning off their **computers**, ready to rejoin the group.

"Want to go get some ice cream?" Pamela asked.

"We just had an ice cream break ourselves," Phil replied, pointing to some empty cups on the table. "But we're happy go with you again."

After their snack, everyone was finally able to get settled into their rooms at the motel. Ali joined Pam and Colette in one room while Nicky, Violet, and Paulina stayed in the room next door. While she was unpacking, Paulina received a text message from Ali, and it **wasn't** good news!

A TERRIBLE LOSS

"Did you see Ali's message?" Paulina asked when the sisters and the ratlets met up outside the motel.

"Yes," Colette replied. "We just texted her back saying that we're going over to meet her!"

"Where is she?" Violet asked.

"In the RV," Pam explained. "She was unpacking her things in our motel room when she started looking through her bag furiously. Then she asked for the keys to the **camper** and scampered off without another squeak!"

Where's Ali?

The Thea Sisters hurried toward the RV and climbed aboard. They found Ali sitting on the floor, her head in her paws.

"I looked everywhere." She sighed, distraught. "The **flash drive** is gone!"

"But that's impossible!" Nicky exclaimed. "You had it in your computer bag this morning. We all saw it!"

"It isn't there anymore!" Ali explained. "And it's not in my **backpack**, either. I looked through all my pockets and it hasn't turned up. After what happened to my laptop, I should have made another **copy** of all the documents, but I kept putting it off! This time, it's entirely my fault."

Pamela tried to reassure her desperate friend.

"Don't blame yourself," Pamela squeaked gently. "This could have happened to anyone. It's not your fault."

"We'll help you look for it," Colette added.

"If it's here, we'll find it!"

The Thea Sisters had no intention of **giving up**. They searched the RV from top to bottom, but they had **no luck**.

"Okay, the flash drive isn't here," Paulina finally admitted. "But let's not lose **hope**. Ali, do you remember when you saw it last?"

Ali thought about it for a moment.

"It was this morning, while I was looking for my sunglasses," she replied.

"Of course, I remember, too!" Colette said, nodding. "You took everything out of your **bag** and placed everything on the steps."

When was the last time you saw it?

"In the rush to get to Cadillac Ranch, maybe you left it on the steps," Violet suggested.

But Pamela had another thought.

"Wait!" she exclaimed. "Remember Andrew, the little **mouse** who was outside the motel? He thought the flash drive was a toy. Maybe, if you left it behind by mistake, he found it and took it thinking you didn't want it!"

"But it sounded like he and his family were **leaving** the motel," Phil pointed out. "They're probably long gone by now."

"True, but that doesn't mean they can't help us," Paulina said, a **mysterious** smile on her snout. Without another word, she scampered out of the RV.

"Phil was right," Paulina explained later. "Andrew and his family did leave their **room** this morning. I explained the situation to the receptionist. She took a look around and the flash drive isn't on the steps. But she is going to try to get in touch with them and give them my phone **number**. Hopefully they'll give me a call and let us know if they have the flash drive!"

That seemed to give Ali some hope. She began pacing back and forth nervously along the length of the camper until Paulina's phone *rang*.

"It must be them!" Paulina squeaked hopefully. "It's a video call!"

Moments later, Andrew's mom appeared on the screen.

"I'm sorry I don't have good news," she said right away. "We left right after meeting you, so it seems unlikely that Andrew took the flash drive.

"But we searched through the car and the **luggage** anyway, just to be sure. We didn't find it!"

"I wanted to find it so I could play with it!" added the little mouse. Then he held up his **stuffed animal** and added, "I'm sorry you lost your unicorn. If you want, I'll let you play with mine!"

"Thank you," Ali replied, trying hard to smile at the sweet gesture. "You're very thoughtful."

Once Ali said good-bye to the little mouse

Sadly, the flash drive isn't here . . .

Thanks anyway!

and his mother, she could no longer hold back her **TEARS**. She turned and ran out of the RV.

CLUE!

ALI'S FLASH DRIVE WAS IN HER SHOULDER BAG WHEN SHE ARRIVED AT THE MOTEL, BUT NOW IT'S GONE! WHERE COULD IT HAVE GONE?

A BiG DECiSioN

"May we come in?" Colette asked as she stood at the door to the MOTEL room.

"Of course, this is your room, too," Ali replied softly as she continued to fold the clothes that had scattered when she had emptied her backpack in search of the flash drive.

"I also tidy up when I need to think," Violet said as she entered the room with the other Thea Sisters. "Cleaning helps me clear my head."

"Oh, but I don't need to think about anything," Ali replied. "I've already made up my mind."

She began placing her folded clothes into her backpack.

The Thea Sisters looked puzzled.

"I've decided to go back to Detroit," Ali finally explained as she continued to pack her bag. "I'm leaving tonight."

"You want to go home?" Pam exclaimed. "But why?!"

I've decided to return to Detroit!

"Why should I stay?" Ali asked, her voice shaky. "That flash drive contained a year's work. Now I've lost all my work! And most of all, I lost the chance to present my video game at Level Up!"

After that

outburst, the Thea Sisters remained silent as they watched their friend pack. How could they make Ali feel better after such a huge **disappointment**? It wouldn't be easy, but maybe they could convince her that they were there for her at such a **difficult** time!

"We can only imagine how sad you must feel," Paulina finally said as she approached Ali. "But we think if you go home now, it will make you feel even **WORSE**! Finish out the trip with us."

"That's true," Nicky added. "Stay with us. Together, we'll see beautiful places, and when you get home, you'll be full of **energy**. You'll be able to get back to work with more enthusiasm!"

Ali sighed deeply and sat down on the bed. "I don't know if I'll ever be able to re-create my video game," she explained.

"Who said you have to remake the same game?" Colette asked as she sat down next to the mouse and put her paw around Ali's shoulders. "Maybe you'll think of a whole new one. An *even better* one!"

"That's right!" Pam joked. "You could use this trip as inspiration. And maybe we'll be the main characters in your new creation!"

Finally, Ali laughed.

Stay with us!

"Actually, that's not a bad idea!" the mouselet replied, smiling.

"Then you have to finish the trip with us," Violet insisted. "That way you can collect a ton of material!"

Ali gave her friends a grateful look and finally accepted.

"Okay, okay, you've **convinced** me," she squeaked. **"I'll stay!"**

After helping Ali unpack her things, Paulina, Nicky, and Violet said good night to the others and went to their room, tired from their **exciting** day. They were just outside the door to their room when they heard two voices they recognized. It was Phil and Jerry. The pair was **HIDDEN** in the dark around the corner of the building, and they were squeaking in whispers.

"Don't worry," Phil was saying. "Nobody will know."

"All right, but make sure you keep your mouth shut!" Jerry replied. "We have to make sure Ali doesn't find out!"

A second later, a door **squeaked** open

and then closed softly. In the silence that followed, the three friends exchanged an alarmed look.

WHAT WAS GOING ON?

CLUE!
WHAT WERE PHIL AND JERRY SECRETLY TALKING ABOUT? WHY DIDN'T THEY WANT TO MAKE ALI SUSPICIOUS?

ARE YOU THINKING
WHAT I'M THINKING?

Paulina, Nicky, and Violet **immediately** wanted to tell the other Thea Sisters what they had overheard. But they didn't want to upset Ali all over again. The mouselets thought their new friend had had enough excitement for one day, and they decided to wait until the next morning to share their news.

"You're right," Colette agreed the next morning when her friends filled her in. "That is really **strange**."

"Are you thinking what I'm thinking?" Pamela asked.

She and the other Thea Sisters were gathered outside the motel.

"Yes, I think so," Violet said, a serious look on her snout. "It seems Phil and Jerry are afraid we'll **find out** about something they did. And the only thing I can think of is that they have something to do with the attack on Ali's computer and the missing flash drive!"

"They certainly have the skills to **hack** a computer," Nicky pointed out.

"And they had plenty of opportunities to nab the **flash drive**," Violet added. "But why would they do that?"

"Maybe they didn't want to go up against Ali in the Level Up competition," Paulina guessed. "Remember when we first met them in St. Louis? They weren't very friendly at first. Maybe they're afraid Ali's project could beat theirs!"

"Well, it's one possibility," Colette agreed.

"But we need **PROOF**. We can't just blame them if we aren't sure."

"You're right, Coco," Paulina agreed. "It's still possible the flash drive simply got lost when Ali went through her **bag**."

We must keep an eye on them!

"We'd better keep an eye on Phil and Jerry," Pam concluded.

"Ready to go?" Ali asked as she, Benji, Phil, and Jerry approached the Thea Sisters.

"We are so ready!" Pamela replied. Then she turned to whisper something softly to Violet. "I think I have an idea!"

Want to drive the RV, Benji?

Pamela walked over to Benji and jingled the KEYS to the RV.

"Hey, Benji, didn't you say you would love to drive an RV?" she asked. "Still interested?"

"Really?!" Benji asked in surprise.

"Of course," Pam agreed, smiling. "I'm happy to drive your CAR for a while!"

A few minutes later, Phil and Jerry settled

themselves in the **back seat** of Benji's car. Pamela got behind the wheel, and Paulina climbed into the front passenger seat next to her friend. She was going to use this opportunity to find out more about Phil and Jerry.

The group set off, and soon they crossed the border into **NEW MEXICO**. As the greenery outside the car window began to change into patches of dry red earth, Paulina sighed deeply.

"I feel so **sorry** for Ali," she lamented. "First the hacker attack, and then her flash drive disappears! What terrible luck!"

As she spoke, Paulina glanced in the rearview mirror. She immediately caught Phil and Jerry exchanging a worried, **uncomfortable** look in the back seat.

"Yeah," Phil said quietly.

"It's too bad," Jerry added.

"It takes a very experienced hacker to break into someone's **computer**, doesn't it?" Pamela asked. "I don't understand much about it, but —"

But she wasn't able to finish her sentence because Phil interrupted her.

"Oh, look!" he exclaimed suddenly. "We're about to enter Santa Rosa. I'll ask the others if they want to stop at the **BLUE HOLE**."

Phil and Jerry texted with the mice in the RV, and the group pulled off the road in Santa Rosa, New Mexico, and headed to the famous Blue Hole. The swimming hole **shimmered** in the middle of the dry desert.

"Phil and Jerry did not want to talk about Ali at all," Paulina told Colette, Nicky, and Violet as they gazed out at the clear, **cool** water.

"Well, we still have a long trip ahead of us," Colette pointed out as she glanced over at Phil and Jerry, who were swimming alongside Ali and Benji. "There will be other chances to find out if our suspicions are correct."

CLUE!
PHIL AND JERRY WERE UNCOMFORTABLE AND CHANGED THE SUBJECT TO AVOID TALKING ABOUT WHAT HAPPENED TO ALI!

MYSTERY IN SANTA FE

After everyone had a chance to swim in the sparkling waters of the Blue Hole, the group got back on the road and continued their journey north. The **heat** gave way to cooler breezes and a landscape of red earth and new expanses of green. They had arrived in **SANTA FE**, the capital of the state of New Mexico!

Without losing sight of Phil and Jerry, the Thea Sisters set out to explore the city, which was so different from those they had seen on their trip.

"What a lovely place!" Violet exclaimed as they arrived at the **Plaza**, the city's central square.

The space was crowded with tourists visiting the small shops, restaurants, and jewelry stalls that lined the streets.

"Look at these beautiful buildings," Ali exclaimed, pointing at the adobe-style architecture, which was so different from the tall skyscrapers they had seen in Chicago. "And the sky is so blue! This would make a picture-perfect postcard. Will you wait for me here while I grab my camera from the RV? I have to take a picture of —"

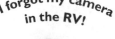

I forgot my camera in the RV!

But Phil interrupted before Ali could finish her sentence.

"I'LL GO!" he exclaimed hastily. "Come with me, Jerry!"

"Huh?!" his friend asked in surprise.

"Let's get Ali's camera for

her from the RV," Phil repeated, staring hard at his friend.

"Uh, right," Jerry finally replied. "Yeah, we'd be happy to."

"But there's no need," Ali reassured them. "I can go get it myself."

They're up to something!

"No, no!" Phil said hurriedly.

"We'll go! I left something in the car, too. Come on, Jerry!"

With that, Phil took the **KEYS** to both vehicles and rushed off with his friend.

The Thea Sisters continued strolling past the shops and art galleries along with Ali and Benji.

MYSTERY in SANTA FE

"It's official: Those two are definitely 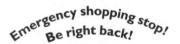hiding something," Nicky whispered to the other Thea Sisters.

Violet nodded. "They jumped at the chance to get into the RV without us!" she agreed quietly.

"Do you think they have a plan?" Pamela whispered in a **worried** voice.

Emergency shopping stop! Be right back!

"I don't know, but I think we should find out," Paulina replied softly. "How do we follow them without Ali and Benji noticing?"

"Leave it to me!" Collette squeaked, winking at her friends. Then she raised her voice so Ali and Benji could hear. "Hey, guys! I'm just going to dash back over to the first stall we saw. I have to get one of those lovely terra-cotta bowls!"

"Do you want us to come with you?" Benji asked.

"No, no!" Colette replied. "Keep on walking. I'll catch up with all of you in a little while."

Colette whirled around and headed back in the direction they had just come from. But instead of stopping at the stall with the terra-cotta bowls, she went to the PARKING LOT.

First Colette made sure Jerry and Phil weren't near their car. Then she scampered quietly up to the RV and peeked in the window. Phil and Jerry were sitting at the table, tinkering with Ali's **LaPtOP**!

Colette gasped, and Phil and Jerry seemed to sense her presence because they both **GLANCED** up and saw her snout at the window. Colette ducked down, but it was too late.

"Colette, wait!" Jerry called out as he poked his head out of the RV.

CLUE!
WHAT ARE PHIL AND JERRY DOING WITH ALI'S COMPUTER?

PHiL AND
JERRY'S TALE

Phil quickly followed his friend out of the RV. They rushed over to Colette.

"Please don't tell Ali that we took her **computer**," Phil said quickly.

"We wanted to surprise her," Jerry added. "But we couldn't fix it!"

Colette was squeakless.

"**SURPRISE HER?**" she asked.

"Yes," Phil explained as he walked back toward the RV. "We wanted to find the files for Ali's **game** and get them back on her computer. Then Ali could have presented her game at the Level Up competition!"

Colette was shocked, and she still had questions.

"But if that's true, why **sneak** around?" Colette asked.

Phil and Jerry looked at each other and sighed.

"Because we weren't sure if we would be able to do it, and we didn't want to get Ali's hopes up," Jerry explained.

"And we also didn't want to look like we were showing off and acting like we know more about computers than Ali does," Phil

We wanted to fix it!

added seriously. "She's an **amazing** computer programmer, you know."

The two mice went on to admit that they initially hadn't been very excited to meet Ali.

"Benji had told us so much about how **talented** Ali is," Phil explained.

"She is an excellent programmer," Jerry added. "So we were nervous about going up against her at Level Up."

Colette smiled.

"Yes, the rest of us noticed that you weren't very warm when we first met you guys," Colette said.

"But once we got to know Ali, everything changed," Jerry said sheepishly. "That little bit of **JEALOUSY** we felt toward Ali turned to great respect!"

"We really were just trying to help," Phil explained.

"After all that's happened the last few days, we were hoping to give Ali a chance to present her game. But once we got on her computer, we realized it was going to be impossible to restore her files!"

"We tried to do it many different ways, but none of them worked!" Jerry admitted, his snout full of disappointment.

"It's true," Phil added with a sigh. "Whoever hacked Ali's laptop was very skilled."

Now that Colette knew the truth, she, Phil, and Jerry returned to the rest of the group. When they arrived in Albuquerque later that night, Colette filled in the other Thea Sisters: Phil and Jerry had not been **to blame** for the attack on Ali's computer. The hacker and the location of the missing flash drive were still a mystery!

All five friends agreed that Jerry and

Phil should tell Ali about how they tried to help. That way there would be no more **SECRETS** between them.

"You're awesome!" Ali exclaimed later at dinner as she leaned over to **hug** the two mice.

"Well, it would have been more awesome if we had been able to fix it," Phil said sadly.

"You've already done so much," Ali assured

Thank you so much!

them. "It was so **thoughtful** of you to try. Wasn't it, Benji?"

"Yes, of course," her friend agreed with a small smile. But he looked **TROUBLED**. "Excuse me," Benji mumbled as he got up suddenly. "I'll be right back."

The mouse scampered to the counter of the restaurant and sat there with his nose buried in one of the menus. He didn't seem to notice that Paulina had watched him leave the table and was now **STUDYING** him carefully. Paulina had noticed that during Phil and Jerry's tale, Benji had kept his eyes down, barely looking at any of them. It also seemed to Paulina that Benji had become flustered and upset when he heard that Phil and Jerry hadn't been able to **fix** Ali's computer.

Paulina knew it wasn't the right time

to share her thoughts with the other Thea Sisters, but she would tell them as soon as she had the chance.

iCE CREAM CONUNDRUM

Was it possible that Benji had something to do with what had happened to Ali's laptop and flash drive? Paulina shared her thoughts

Suspect?

with her friends later that evening, and all five friends agreed that Phil, Jerry, and Benji likely had the skills to hack a **computer.** But at the same time, Benji had been Ali's friend since school, and the Thea Sisters knew Ali **trusted** him. The friends had trouble believing he could have done this to his good friend!

Still, the Thea Sisters noticed that after the evening in Albuquerque, Benji became much quieter and seemed to hang back by himself whenever he could.

Meanwhile, the journey along ROUTE 66 continued. The group crossed the border between New Mexico and Arizona and entered the city of Flagstaff.

We're in Arizona!

The next day, the mouselets had planned a detour to visit the **GRAND CANYON**. Determined to relax after the many stops they had made the previous days, the Thea Sisters sat outside at a table at their motel to update their trip album.

"Let's start by choosing photos to print," Paulina suggested. She arranged the mini travel printer in front of her.

"I'd love to save a page for the Painted Desert in Petrified Forest National Park," Colette said as she scrolled through the photos on her phone. "I'm sure I got a good photo when we were there. It was so **beautiful!**"

But a few minutes later, Colette gave up. None of her photos had turned out as well as she thought they did.

"I think I may have taken a few while we

were there," Phil said. He, Ali, and Jerry had just joined the group. He handed his **cell phone** to Nicky and tapped on a folder. "Here's where I keep my photos."

"This one is **perfect**!" Nicky exclaimed when she got to one of the images. "Thanks, Phil, you saved the day!"

"No problem," Phil said with a smile. "If you see any other photos you want to use, I'd be happy to **share** them with you."

The Thea Sisters began flipping through his photo gallery. Pam stopped when she got to a funny selfie of Phil and Jerry holding three giant cups of ice cream.

"It looks like you were really hungry for some **ice cream** in this shot!" Pam said with a chuckle.

Jerry burst out laughing.

"They weren't all for us! That was in Amarillo. The third cup was for Benji. He stayed back in the **RV**!"

The Thea Sisters perked up their ears.

"So Benji stayed in the **RV**?" Paulina repeated slowly.

"Yes," Phil confirmed. "He had to finish updating his computer, so we went to buy ice cream for the three of us. We went to that great ICE CREAM PLACE we all went to together later on, remember?"

The friends nodded.

The pieces of the puzzle were starting to fit together. Once they were alone, the Thea Sisters continued to talk about it.

"Let's go over things just to be sure," Violet said. "When we arrived in Amarillo, our motel rooms weren't ready yet. So Ali left her **luggage** in the RV along with her computer bag."

"Right," Colette agreed, nodding. "That was the night Ali noticed that her **flash drive** was missing."

"And it was the same day that Benji was left alone in the RV while Phil and Jerry went to buy **ice cream**," Nicky concluded thoughtfully.

Was it possible that Benji had hacked into Ali's computer and then stolen her flash drive?

Even though they truly hoped they were wrong, the Thea Sisters began to think they'd figured it out!

SUMMARY OF CLUES:

1) WHOEVER HACKED ALI'S COMPUTER WAS AN EXPERIENCED COMPUTER PROGRAMMER.

2) BENJI WAS LEFT ALONE IN THE RV WITH THE FLASH DRIVE WHILE HIS FRIENDS WENT TO BUY ICE CREAM.

3) FROM THE TIME HE FOUND OUT THAT PHIL AND JERRY HAD TRIED TO HELP ALI, BENJI HAD BECOME VERY QUIET.

SHOWDOWN AT THE GRAND CANYON

The following morning, the group of travelers set off for the place they were all most excited about: **GRAND CANYON NATIONAL PARK**! While they enjoyed the beautiful view of the gorge carved by the **Colorado River**, the Thea Sisters were determined to talk to Benji and see if they were right. But getting him to talk to them was going to be hard, as Benji seemed **quieter** than ever!

Throughout their hike, Benji walked **apart** from the group, always a few steps ahead or behind the other mice. Then after one sharp turn in the trail, Pamela realized that Benji had disappeared!

"Hey, wait a minute!" Pamela exclaimed as

she stopped suddenly on the trail. "Where's Benji?!"

Ali looked around her in surprise.

"He was right behind us just a few minutes ago!" she said.

"Well, I don't see him anywhere," Paulina said in alarm. "I say we go back and **LOOK** for him."

We have to talk with Benji!
Yes!

"Let's split up," Nicky suggested. "Ali, Phil, and Jerry, you continue on ahead. The rest of us will go back the direction we came."

So the group split in two and the Thea Sisters began to retrace their steps along the trail. Before too long, they spotted Benji's colorful **T-shirt** ahead of them. The mouse was standing at one of the lookouts along the trail, his paws sunk deep into his pockets and his eyes fixed straight ahead, a serious look on his snout.

"**There you are!**" Colette exclaimed. "We were worried about you."

Startled, Benji jumped and turned toward his friends. Then without a squeak, he turned back to look out at the horizon. The mouse's eyes were filled with **TEARS.**

"Hey, Benji, are you okay?" Violet asked softly as she approached him.

"I'm fine!" Benji replied gruffly.

"Do you want us to call Ali for you?" Nicky suggested.

"**NO!**" Benji replied, almost shouting. "Why would you call her?"

"Because Ali is a good friend of yours," Pamela answered. "If there's something wrong, maybe you would feel more comfortable talking to her instead of us."

Benji **sighed**.

"I don't think I'll ever feel comfortable with her again," he explained. "Not after what I did to her."

Benji was silent for a few moments, but then he opened up to the Thea Sisters. As they looked out over one of the most beautiful **views** in the world, Benji told his five new friends what had **REALLY** happened.

"A few weeks ago, I heard from an old

friend in Detroit," Benji began. "He told me that Ali was going to present a **video game** at Level Up. When she agreed to stop in St. Louis, I was so glad to see her again.

"But when I realized her video game was created from the idea we had together, I got jealous."

He hung his head and continued his tale.

Benji, there you are!

"I felt even worse when I realized her project was great! I had always known Ali was a talented programmer, but . . ."

Benji trailed off.

"But overnight, your childhood friend had turned into a rival?" Paulina said.

"Yes," Benji confirmed.

"But Ali wanted you to work with her on

I didn't behave like a friend at all . . .

the Power Princess project!" Violet pointed out. "You were the one who told her no."

"I know," Benji admitted. "The truth is, I didn't even remember that conversation. When Ali and I talked, I was so involved with my new friends in St. Louis, I barely paid any attention."

I wanted to fix it...

"Did you crash Ali's **computer**?" Paulina asked.

Benji nodded slowly.

"And did you take the **flash drive** where she had saved the only backup copy of her work?" Colette chimed in.

"Yes," Benji admitted. "It was me. But I felt bad right away and I wanted to fix it!

CRACK!
CRACK!

It's just —"

Benji was interrupted by the sound of twigs **snapping**. Benji and the Thea Sisters turned to see Ali standing just a few yards

Benji connected to the Wi-Fi network and hacked into Ali's computer, causing it to crash . . .

. . . then he stole her flash drive with the backup copy of her program!

away, staring at her friend with a look of **disbelief** on her snout.

"Ali!" Benji exclaimed. "I'm so sorry . . ."

But before Benji could finish his sentence, Ali had turned and scampered off.

A BROKEN HEART

Ali had always considered Benji one of her closest friends. Finding out that he was the one who ruined her Level Up project had **broken** her heart. Ali stopped and sat down on a big boulder. Tears began to flow down her cheeks.

The Thea Sisters stood beside her quietly, hugging her tightly. There wasn't much they could say or do to make her feel better, but they hoped just being there would comfort their friend.

After a while, the group of friends headed back to the RV. Benji was there waiting for them, his eyes downcast and a look of **embarrassment** on his snout.

"I know you don't want to talk to me, Ali," Benji said to his friend. "I get it. But I have something to give you."

Benji slipped his paw into the pocket of his jeans and pulled out the **unicorn** flash drive Ali had used to store her video game

We're here for you, Ali!

backup. The flash drive was broken and useless.

"I figured you had gotten rid of it by now," Ali said in surprise when she saw it.

"No. When the others found me at the overlook, I was trying to find the courage to throw it away," Benji said. "But in the end, I couldn't do it. I BROKE it, but I couldn't get rid of it completely."

As Ali listened with a stern look on her snout, Benji tried to explain why he had done what he did.

"I wasn't thinking clearly," Benji admitted. "I regretted it, but by then it was TOO LATE."

"That's why you became so quiet after you learned that Phil and Jerry had tried to fix Ali's computer," Paulina pointed out.

"Yes," Benji agreed. "I felt so guilty knowing how badly I had behaved. I couldn't

laugh or joke around with anyone anymore. Ali, I don't know if you can ever forgive me, but let me at least try to **make it up** to you!"

Ali looked at her old friend, her paws crossed over her chest.

"I don't see how you could ever make this right," she said.

"The drive is broken, but I think I may still be able to **recover** the contents," Benji said.

"Why should I trust you now?" Ali shouted, still very upset by what Benji had done.

"Because I realize how wrong I was, and I would like to be your friend again," Benji explained. "I already talked to Phil and Jerry. I'm not going to present our game with them. Instead, I can use my free time to work with you so that you'll be ready to present Power Princess at the competition!"

"But we don't have enough time," Ali lamented. "We will be on the road for the next couple of days. When and how are we going to find time to WORK?!"

"Actually, if we leave now and don't make any more STOPS, it should take about a day to get to California," Pamela pointed out.

I want to fix things!

"What about your trip along Route 66?" Ali asked, astonished. "If we leave for California right now, you won't get to make all the stops you had planned on your vacation!"

Nicky smiled.

"This **TRIP** has already given us a lot more than we expected, now that we're going home with four new friends!"

"And knowing that we helped you would make us very **happy**," Violet added.

"What do you say?" Benji asked hopefully. "Shall we give it a try?" He held out the flash drive to his friend in his open paw. Ali stared intently at the small object that held all that was left of her work. Then she looked at Benji and the Thea Sisters.

Finally, a small smile crept across her snout.

"Okay," she said.

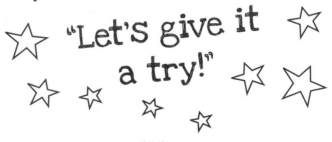

"Let's give it a try!"

WE'RE A TEAM!

Once the decision had been made, they changed their route and headed straight for **SAN FRANCISCO** the next morning. From the moment they left, Ali and Benji set to work in a studio the Thea Sisters had created especially for them. The tiny RV's living room had been turned into a fully operational **WORKSTATION!**

Once they arrived in San Francisco, the two young programmers continued to work **NONSTOP** for hours. Meanwhile, the Thea Sisters spent their time exploring the beautiful city overlooking the San Francisco Bay.

"This trip began with a change of plans and ended with another **CHANGE OF PLANS**!" Colette said with a laugh as she, Nicky, Pam, Paulina, and Violet returned to the small house they were staying at with the others. "But it's been a wonderful adventure!"

"Yes, and I don't regret leaving Route 66 for San Francisco," Pamela said. "This city is **fabumouse!**"

"I wonder if Ali and Benji are done yet,"

New schedule . . . new city!

Paulina said. "The presentation is tomorrow!"

"We can just ask," Violet said. "Look, there Benji is now!"

Sure enough, Benji was heading down the sidewalk toward them.

"Where are you going with that **backpack**?" Nicky asked him.

Benji just grinned.

"I'm going **home**," he said. "Ali and I finished, so there's no reason for me to stay."

"You're not staying for the presentation?" Colette asked. "Don't you want to know how it turns out?"

Benji shook his head.

"I don't need to stay," he explained, his smile widening. "I know it's going to be **GREAT**!"

Benji said good-bye to his new friends and then turned and scampered quickly down the block. A moment later, the door to the house swung open and Ali HURRIED down the steps.

"Mouselets, I'm so glad you're here!" she exclaimed when she saw the Thea Sisters.

"Did you happen to see Benji?"

"Yes, he just left a minute ago," Paulina explained. "He said he was heading home."

"He went that way," Violet added, pointing down the street.

Ali quickly took off in the direction Violet had pointed. The Thea Sisters hurried after her. A few minutes later, the group saw Benji as he was about to enter the SUBWAY station.

"Benji, WAIT!" Ali called out to her friend. Benji turned.

"What's up?" he asked.

"You can't just leave!" Ali exclaimed.
"Don't you want to be there when I present
Power Princess tomorrow?!"

Benji looked at her in surprise.

Did you see Benji?

He went that way...

"After what I've done?" he asked. "I was sure you wouldn't **want me** there!"

"Yes, that was wrong, but I have decided to forgive you," Ali said. "I would never have been able to redo all the work by myself."

It's your project . . .

But you helped!

"That's why I really want to give you a second chance, Benji. You're still my friend, and you did the right thing in the end. I forgive you, and I want you to be at the presentation to support me. Will you come?"

Benji considered Ali's offer for a few moments before he nodded and smiled.

"OKay, I'm in," he said. "I'll be there for you tomorrow!"

"Awesome!" Pam said cheerfully. "We'll accompany you both to San Jose tomorrow!"

As a light rain began to fall, the group of friends headed inside, ready to face the last stage of their incredible adventure together!

THE BIG DAY

The next morning, the Thea Sisters went with Ali and Benji to the presentation in **Silicon Valley**. But because they could not go inside with the contestants, they waited for their friends on the lawn in front of the building.

"Okay, who wants to play?" Nicky asked as she pulled a FLYING DISK out of her backpack.

Violet frowned.

"Right here?" she asked. "In front of Level Up?!"

"Sure, why not?" Nicky asked. "I can't stop thinking about Ali's presentation and how it's going. I need to move to **DiStract** myself!"

"**That's not a bad idea!**" Pamela agreed, and she got up from the bench where she had been sitting. "Who's on my TEAM?"

The five friends began to pass the flying disk back and forth. Suddenly, they were interrupted by a male voice behind them.

"Can we join you?"

"Phil! Jerry!" Colette exclaimed as she ran

over to the two mice. "How did it go?"

"It went well!" Phil replied. "They said our project has potential, though it still needs some work."

"They gave us some great tips on ways to make it better," Jerry added. "We agreed to show it to them again as soon as we make some **changes**."

Good work, mice!

"That's really great news!" Pamela said as she gave Phil a high five. "Well done!"

"Do you know anything about Ali's project?" Violet asked.

"Have you seen her and Benji?"

"I think the Power Princess presentation is happening right now," Jerry said with a smile. "If you don't mind, we'd like to **WAIT** for them with you!"

The wait didn't last long. Less than ten minutes later, Ali and Benji emerged from the building.

"Tell me those smiles mean what I'm hoping they mean," Pamela exclaimed as she scampered over to greet them.

Ali and Benji exchanged a quick smile and then shouted in unison: "**YES!**"

Surrounded by their friends, the pair told them about how Ali's project had thrilled the Level Up team.

"Ali was great," Benji said, his eyes **SHINING** with pride. "Her presentation was exciting and smart!"

"They've asked me to move to San Jose to work on the development of the video game!" Ali said.

"Next week Ali has an appointment with the Level Up **programmers** to refine the details," Benji explained. "But it looks like Power Princess is on the road to becoming a real video game!"

"Amazing!" the Thea Sisters cheered.

Ali did it!

"I don't know about the rest of you, but I really couldn't have imagined a better ending to this trip," Colette said as she **hugged** her friends.

"Neither could I," Ali replied, moved by the love and support of her friends.

"I'm also grateful that things worked out so well in the end,"

Benji said. "I almost made a real mess of things for Ali. But thanks to her hard work, and her forgiveness, now I know for sure that she's a true

♕ **POWER** ♕
PRINCESS!"

THE FIVE DUCHESSES

For the Thea Sisters, the day after the presentation also happened to be the last day of their **ROAD TRIP**. It was time for the five friends to say good-bye to Ali, Benji, Phil, and Jerry and return to Mouseford Academy.

"Here we are," Ali announced as she parked outside the San Francisco airport.

"Thanks for the ride," Nicky replied as they unloaded their bags.

Ali smiled.

"It seems like that's the least I could do after you let me ride in your **RV** with you all the way from Pontiac!"

"Traveling together all those miles was a lot of fun!" Pam said, smiling.

"Without you, our **ROAD TRIP** wouldn't have been the same!"

"We're so looking forward to playing your **video game** when it comes out," Paulina said as she put on her backpack.

"Speaking of which . . ." Benji smiled as he handed Paulina a blue **FOLDER**. "Here's a little **PREVIEW** you might enjoy!"

"I'll be waiting to hear what you think," Ali added with a **wink** at her friends.

After hugging their traveling buddies one last time, the **THEA SISTERS** set off toward their gate. While they were waiting to get on their flight home, they decided to open the folder with the plans for Ali's video game.

"It looks like fun!" Pam said. "The **PRINCESS** has to go through a lot of trials to free her prince!"

For you!

"Hey, wait a second," said Nicky as she turned to a page entitled **The Five Duchesses.**

"It's us!" Colette exclaimed excitedly as she recognized herself and her friends in the drawings.

The drawings showed five characters in the **video game** who help the princess carry out her mission.

The Five Duchesses

"I never dreamed of becoming a character in a video game!" Paulina squeaked with delight.

Violet smiled.

"This just shows the power of friendship," she said. "It makes dreams come true,

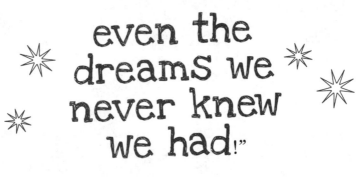

even the dreams we never knew we had!"

Don't miss any of these exciting Thea Sisters adventures!

Thea Stilton and the
Dragon's Code

Thea Stilton and the
Mountain of Fire

Thea Stilton and the
Ghost of the Shipwreck

Thea Stilton and the
Secret City

Thea Stilton and the
Mystery in Paris

Thea Stilton and the
Cherry Blossom Adventure

Thea Stilton and the
Star Castaways

Thea Stilton: Big Trouble
in the Big Apple

Thea Stilton and the
Ice Treasure

Thea Stilton and the
Secret of the Old Castle

Thea Stilton and the
Blue Scarab Hunt

Thea Stilton and the
Prince's Emerald

Thea Stilton and the
Mystery on the Orient Express

Thea Stilton and the
Dancing Shadows

Thea Stilton and the
Legend of the Fire Flowers

Thea Stilton and the
Spanish Dance Mission

**Thea Stilton and the
Journey to the Lion's Den**

**Thea Stilton and the
Great Tulip Heist**

**Thea Stilton and the
Chocolate Sabotage**

**Thea Stilton and the
Missing Myth**

**Thea Stilton and the
Lost Letters**

**Thea Stilton and the
Tropical Treasure**

**Thea Stilton and the
Hollywood Hoax**

**Thea Stilton and the
Madagascar Madness**

**Thea Stilton and the
Frozen Fiasco**

**Thea Stilton and the
Venice Masquerade**

**Thea Stilton and the
Niagara Splash**

**Thea Stilton and the
Riddle of the Ruins**

**Thea Stilton and the
Phantom of the Orchestra**

**Thea Stilton and the
Black Forest Burglary**

**Thea Stilton and the
Race for the Gold**

**Thea Stilton and the
Rainforest Rescue**

**Thea Stilton and the
American Dream**

31901066421068